HEY GOD, I'M SORRY TO BE STUBBORN, BUT I JUST DON'T LIKE ANYONE RIDING ON MY BACK!

THE DONKEY
TELLS HIS SIDE OF
THE STORY

TROY SCHMIDT
ILLUSTRATED BY CORY JONES

PEOPLE SAY I'M STUBBORN. I'M NOT.

I JUST DON'T LIKE PEOPLE ON MY BACK.

THAT'S WHAT HAPPENS WHEN YOU'RE A DONKEY.

PEOPLE THINK THEY CAN JUST CLIMB

ON BOARD AND GO FOR A RIDE.

LIKE WHEN THIS GUY NAMED JESUS CAME TO TOWN . . .

LET ME TELL YOU MY SIDE OF THE STORY.

THIS IS MY MOM. WE ALWAYS HANG OUT TOGETHER.
BUT I THINK I EMBARRASS HER IN PUBLIC . . .
ESPECIALLY WHEN I THROW MY TEMPER TANTRUMS.
OKAY, MAYBE I'M A LITTLE SENSITIVE.

YOU SEE, THESE PEOPLE WHO OWN US THINK THEY CAN JUST THROW THESE HEAVY SACKS ON OUR BACKS. WHAT DO THEY THINK I AM . . . THEIR BEAST OF BURDEN?! SO WHEN THEY DO, I TEND TO FREAK OUT A BIT. HHHEEEEEEEEEEEEEEE-HHHHAAAAAAAAAAAAAAAAAWWWWWW! AND I KICK THE SACK OFF MY BACK.

THEN THEY THINK THEY CAN JUST CLIMB ON MY BACK AND GO FOR A RIDE. HHHEEEEEEEEEEEEE-HHHHAAAAAAAAAAAWWWW! WHAT DO I LOOK LIKE? A HORSEY? DO YOU KNOW HOW HEAVY THESE PEOPLE ARE? AND THEY WANT TO RIDE FOR HOURS . . . UPHILL! THIS IS WHY WE DONKEYS HAVE LOWER BACK PAIN.

MOM ONCE SAID TO ME, "WHY ARE YOU ACTING
THIS WAY? WE HAVE TO CARRY THESE PEOPLE
AND THEIR THINGS. IT'S WHAT DONKEYS DO."
"THEN MAYBE I'M IN THE WRONG LINE OF WORK!"
I SCREAMED. "I'M GOING ON STRIKE!"
SO FROM THEN ON, ANYTHING THAT TOUCHED MY BACK,
I KICKED IT OFF. A MAN, A WOMAN, A CHILD, A BIRD, EVEN A FLY.
"DON'T TOUCH ME! I'M ON STRIKE!"
HHHEEEEEEEEEEEEE-HHHHAAAAAAAAAAAWWWWW!

MOM SHOOK HER HEAD.
"YOU HAVE TO DO WHAT YOU WERE MADE TO DO.
BUT IF YOU DON'T LET ANYONE ON YOUR BACK,
THEY'LL GET RID OF YOU."
GET RID OF ME? BUT ... THAT'S THE WAY I AM.
SOMEBODY NEEDS TO STAND UP FOR THE
MISTREATMENT OF DONKEYS ALL OVER THE WORLD!
NO MORE SACKS ON OUR BACKS!

THE NEXT DAY, TWO MEN WALKED INTO TOWN AND TALKED TO MY BOSS.
"WE'RE LOOKING FOR A DONKEY AND A YOUNG COLT THAT HAS NOT BEEN RIDDEN."
NOW THAT WAS WEIRD. WHO WANTS A YOUNG DONKEY THAT NO ONE HAS RIDDEN?
MY OWNER POINTED AT ME. "THERE'S ONE RIGHT HERE.
NO ONE HAS EVER RIDDEN THIS ONE. YOU CAN HAVE HIM FOR FREE!"
IF THESE GUYS THINK THEY'RE GOING TO TAKE ME FOR A RIDE,
THEY'VE GOT A SURPRISE COMING.

"WHO NEEDS IT?" MY OWNER ASKED.
THE MEN RESPONDED, "THE LORD."
AND THEN I KNEW THAT MOM WAS RIGHT.
THEY WERE GOING TO GET RID OF ME.
THEY WERE GOING TO SEND ME AWAY.
AND SENDING ME TO "THE LORD"
COULD ONLY MEAN ONE THING:
I WAS ABOUT TO SEE GOD. *GULP!*

SO I PRAYED, "HEY, GOD, I'M SORRY I'VE BEEN A STUBBORN DONKEY,
BUT I JUST DON'T LIKE ANYONE RIDING ON MY BACK!"
GOD ANSWERED BACK, "I KNOW HOW YOU ARE,
BUT I WANT YOU TO BE MORE HELPFUL.
SOMETIMES YOU HAVE TO SACRIFICE TO HELP OTHERS.
CARRYING OTHERS ON YOUR BACK IS WHAT I MADE YOU TO DO."
"I WILL! I WILL!" I CRIED. "I WON'T BE THAT WAY EVER AGAIN.
PLEASE DON'T SEND ME AWAY FOREVER."

"THEN I HAVE A VERY IMPORTANT JOB FOR YOU.
I WANT YOU TO CARRY SOMEONE VERY SPECIAL TO ME,
MY SON.
PEOPLE LONG AGO IN THE SCRIPTURES SAID HE
WOULD RIDE A YOUNG DONKEY INTO TOWN
THAT NOBODY HAD EVER RIDDEN,
THAT DONKEY IS YOU."
"THE SCRIPTURES? PEOPLE KNEW ABOUT ME
IN THE SCRIPTURES? HOW CAN THAT BE?
I'M JUST A STUBBORN DONKEY ON STRIKE."
GOD REPLIED, "YOU'RE STILL VERY IMPORTANT TO ME."

THE TWO MEN TOOK US TO ANOTHER MAN.
THEY CALLED HIM JESUS. HE HAD A GENTLE SMILE
AND A WARMTH ABOUT HIM THAT CALMED ME.
"HERE ARE THE DONKEYS YOU REQUESTED, MASTER,"
THE MEN SAID. "THIS ONE HAS NEVER BEEN RIDDEN.
THE OWNERS SAID HE'S VERY STUBBORN AND
KICKS OFF WHOEVER TRIES TO RIDE HIM."

OH NO! MY SECRET WAS OUT. I KNEW HE WAS GOING TO REJECT ME AND SEND ME AWAY TOO. BUT JESUS PETTED ME ON THE NOSE. HE SAID, "NO, HE'LL DO JUST FINE. THIS IS THE ONE I'VE BEEN WAITING FOR. THIS IS THE ONE THE PROPHETS SPOKE OF." ME?! GOD'S SON WAS WAITING FOR A STUBBORN OL' DONKEY LIKE ME!

SO I ENDED MY STRIKE AND ALLOWED JESUS TO CLIMB ON MY BACK. THAT VERY DAY, WE RODE INTO JERUSALEM FOR A HUGE PARADE. AND GUESS WHO WAS THE MAIN ATTRACTION . . . JESUS! AND I GOT TO BE WITH HIM. EVEN THOUGH I HAD REJECTED SO MANY PEOPLE BEFORE, JESUS DIDN'T REJECT ME.

THIS JESUS, I LATER HEARD, SACRIFICED HIS LIFE FOR EVERYONE IN THE WORLD. THE LEAST I COULD DO IS CARRY OTHERS FOR HIM. AND FROM THEN ON, I CARRIED PEOPLE ON MY BACK WHEREVER THEY WANTED TO GO. SOOO, ANYONE WANT A RIDE? IT'S THE LEAST THIS BEAST COULD DO FOR GOD.